Utterly Flutterly Fairies

Freya
the
Fashion Fairy

Freya
the
Fashion Fairy

Moira Butterfield

Illustrated by Liz and Kate Pope

Potter
BOOKS

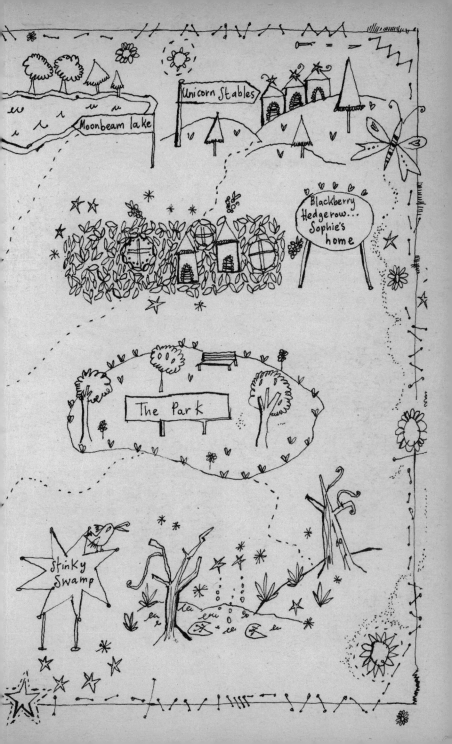

Meet the Utterly Flutterly Fairies!

Freya the Fashion Fairy

Special spells in her backpack

Clever weather magic dust
The power to make a rainbow

Magic beauty jewel
The power to create beautiful clothes

A good feeling spell ring
The power to give someone a happy thought

Freya's special skill
*She is able to camouflage herself,
so people don't see her*

Daisy the Dream Fairy

Special spells in her backpack

Clever weather magic dust
The power to calm storms

Magic beauty jewel
The power to create starlight

A good feeling spell ring
The power to make everything taste dreamy

Daisy's special skill
*She is able to fly very fast
and she is good at sport*

Clara the Clever Fairy

Special spells in her backpack

Clever weather magic dust
*The power to create a gentle breeze
(No wonder her Dad is always
inventing new kinds of windmill
to help run their home)*

Magic beauty jewel
The power to change colours

A good feeling spell ring
The power to give someone a bright idea

Clara's special skill
*She can make objects move a little (she's still
learning how to make them move a lot). She
can also magically see where things are broken*

Sophie the Birthday Fairy

Special spells in her backpack

Clever weather magic dust
The power to conjure up some sunshine

Magic beauty jewel
The power to make someone hear beautiful music

A good feeling spell ring
The power to put a smile on someone's face

Sophie's special skill
*She is especially good at looking after
animals, and can talk their languages*

And watch out for. . .

Drizzle the Wicked Witch

She would just love to get her hands on the fairies' spells, with the help of her mean and horrible sidekicks, the Craggy Crows!

More Utterly Flutterly Fun!

*Look out for the pages of Utterly Flutterly
Fairy Fun at the end of this book.*

**Bake beautiful
butterfly cakes**

**Make a fairy
friendship bracelet**

**Have a go at
our fairy quiz**

**Make a brilliant
butterfly clip**

Written by Moira Butterfield
Designed by Tracey Cunnell
Edited by Pat Hegarty
Illustrated by Liz and Kate Pope

Created by WizzBook Ltd

First published in the UK
by Potter Books, RH17 5PA, UK

www.potterbooks.co.uk

Printed in the UK by CPI Bookmarque, Croydon, CR0 4TD

Chapter 1
Freya Starts a Trend

The next time you go to your school, look carefully around the playground. Is there a quiet spot in a corner? Could something small, secret and magical be hiding there? I heard that in a hole in a tree, on the edge of somebody's school playground, there was a very special secret indeed – the *Utterly Flutterly Fairy School*! I don't know which playground it's in. It could be yours. If you spot it, keep it a secret, won't you?

Little fairies arrive at the fairy school every morning, just after the human children have gone indoors.

Freya the Fashion Fairy gets a lift on the back of her beautiful pet butterfly, Shimmerwing.

Come on, Shimmerwing!

One morning before school, Freya and Shimmerwing were playing together in the flower garden where they live. The weather was dull and grey. Freya gave a big sigh.

"The sky is all dirty-coloured. I'd like to think of a way to brighten things up."

She watched as Shimmerwing flitted around, his rainbow-coloured wings glittering as he moved.

Then she chuckled. "Thank you, Shimmerwing! You've just given me a great idea!"

She rummaged in her school backpack, where she kept her collection of special Fashion Fairy spells.

"This will do the trick," she grinned, bringing out her Magic Beauty Jewel, which had the power to make new fashions and change clothes. She rubbed it gently and chanted some magic words:

"Make some tiny Shimmerwings,
To clip on everybody's things."

Four brightly-coloured clips appeared, decorated to look like pretty butterflies. Freya fixed one on to her backpack.

15

"A new fashion is born! Let's go to school, and make it more cool!" she laughed with her tinkly fairy laugh.

At school Freya gave a butterfly clip to each of her three special friends – Clara, Sophie and Daisy. Everybody who saw them loved them, so at breaktime she made lots more.

Even the head teacher, Mrs Daffodil, asked for a clip to decorate her bag.

"Thank you, Freya. These beautiful mini butterflies will cheer everyone up," she smiled.

She wasn't the only one to notice Freya's new fashion trend. A couple of Craggy Crows saw what was going on as they hid on a nearby branch. They'd been sent to spy by Drizzle the Wicked Witch. When they saw all the pupils wearing mini butterflies, they flew off to her hideout in Stinky Swamp to give her the news.

Drizzle was busy throwing rotten, smelly eggs into her cauldron of magic potion. No matter what yucky stuff she stirred in, the potion usually stayed weak and useless. Drizzle never understood why, but, in fact, it was thanks to a clever secret spell put on the cauldron by Mrs Daffodil.

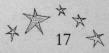

Drizzle's potion *sometimes* got stronger, but only when there was chaos and muddle in the human world. Even then its power didn't last long. No wonder she was always so bad-tempered.

The crows told her all about the new fashion for colourful clips sweeping the fairy school.

"So stupid," she sneered. "I hate colour. Silly fairies and humans like it because it makes them happy. How pathetic!"

Her eyes narrowed.

"I've just thought of the perfect plan for making them *unhappy*," she screeched, and for once she smiled.

Chapter 2
A Dressing Disaster!

News of Freya's fashion trend had given the witch a particularly mean idea, and she explained it to her Craggy Crows. A group of them soon appeared, lurking outside the clothes shop in the bustling human town.

"There are lots of crows outside today," the shopkeeper remarked, but she didn't have time to think about it much because she was very busy. There was a sale on, and she was taking money and putting

clothes in bags for her customers. Once the shoppers carried the bags outside, the Craggy Crows went into action.

"Squawk!"

One crow would screech, distracting a shopper, while another crow flew down and quickly pecked at the clothes in the shopping bags.

By the afternoon, the poor shopkeeper was being rushed off her feet, not by shoppers buying new clothes, but by people coming back to complain. When they'd got home they'd found holes and rips in their new outfits.

The fairy friends had no idea what was going on. As they headed home from school together, a little bee started flying around them, buzzing madly. Sophie the Birthday Fairy knew how to talk to

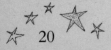

animals, so she soon found out what the trouble was.

"The bee says there are lots of humans getting angry outside the clothes shop in the town. He thinks it's something to do with the Craggy Crows. We'd better go and find out."

When the fairies arrived at the shop they saw a crowd of angry customers queuing up to complain. The fairies flew quietly in through the back door and hid behind a vase of flowers, to listen to what was going on.

"My new dress has holes in it. Look!" complained one customer.

"My skirt has got so many rips, it's almost as if a bird has pecked it," added another.

"I'll sort this out," Freya muttered angrily. "Can one of you distract the shoppers for a minute or two?"

Sophie the Birthday Fairy nodded. "Can do!"

She flew around to the front of the shop, took out her Birthday Fairy Magic Beauty Jewel, and chanted a little spell:

"I'll make some music with my jewel,
To stop the crows from being so cruel."

Wonderful dance music floated through the air. The shoppers tapped their toes, put down their damaged clothes and began to dance!

"It feels as if my feet are enchanted!" someone laughed. "I can dance as light as a fairy!"

Quickly, Freya took out her Fashion Fairy Beauty Jewel and used its magic to mend all the holes and tears the crows had made with their beaks. By the time the music stopped, everything looked perfect again.

"That's odd," the shoppers mumbled. They went home a bit puzzled, but with outfits as good as new.

"Phew! That was a muddle and a half," Freya sighed. She sat down on the shelf, put down her jewel and yawned.

"Let's go home. I'm exhausted!"

The shopkeeper had a little girl, and later on that day she noticed something shiny on the shelf.

"Can I have this, Mum?" she asked.

"Yes, of course. I've never seen it before," her mum agreed.

And the little girl slipped Freya's forgotten Magic Beauty Jewel into her pocket!

Chapter 3
A Nasty Surprise!

Back in Stinky Swamp, Drizzle's magic potion had begun to bubble. She cackled happily to her Craggy Crows.

"The pecking worked a treat. You made the humans unhappy and you made a lovely big muddle. Now my potion is strong enough to do some really mean magic!"

The very next morning Freya found out just how mean Drizzle could be. During the night, poor, beautiful Shimmerwing

had turned grey all over! It wasn't an ordinary grey either. It was dirty and smeary-looking.

"It's a witchy colour!" gasped Freya.

The other little garden creatures had all lost their colours, too.

"I'll find a way to help you all, I promise," Freya cried angrily. But, even as she spoke, the garden flowers began to turn grey as well!

There was no time to lose. Freya jumped on to the back of Shimmerwing, flew as fast as she could to school, and burst into Mrs Daffodil's office. Clara, Daisy and Sophie ran in behind her. They'd seen their friend arrive on her unhappy grey pet and they were very worried.

"Drizzle has turned the colour off!" she cried.

"Where? When?" her friends gasped.

"Tell me exactly what has happened," Mrs Daffodil said gently.

Freya pointed out of the window to the miserable Shimmerwing.

"Everything in my garden is turning grey," she sobbed. "It's terrible!"

"Hmm, that sounds mean enough to be witch magic," Mrs Daffodil replied. "Has something happened to make Drizzle's potion stronger?"

Freya told Mrs Daffodil about the birds pecking the clothes and upsetting the humans.

Mrs Daffodil nodded. "That will have created enough unhappiness to make Drizzle's potion more powerful. I'm guessing she could have mixed it with a colour-draining spell, then flown across during the night and sprinkled it all over your garden."

"I can help," Clara piped up. "My Clever Fairy Magic Beauty Jewel can change colours. Look!" She took her jewel from her backpack, rubbed it and pointed at Shimmerwing.

"Turn Shimmerwing back from grey,
And push the witch's spell away."

Instantly, Shimmerwing's shiny rainbow colours reappeared, and Freya gave her clever friend a delighted hug.

"Freya, take Clara to your garden, straight away, to put things right," Mrs Daffodil said. So the two fairy friends sped off to Freya's home, and Clara started turning things back to their usual colours.

But, as quickly as she turned one flower back, another went grey.

"I can't keep up," Clara sighed sadly. "This colour-draining spell is strong and it's spreading!" They flew back to the Utterly Flutterly School, and all the way there they saw flowers turning grey below them. When they told Mrs Daffodil she looked grim.

"At this rate, the humans will soon see there's something wrong," she muttered. "If they start to panic, their unhappiness will make Drizzle's bad magic stronger and stronger."

Freya moaned. "I couldn't stand it if the whole world went grey. Mrs Daffodil, can't you stop it?"

Mrs Daffodil replied thoughtfully, "I could only work out how to reverse

such a bad spell if I had a few drops of Drizzle's magic potion."

"But the potion is in the cauldron, in scary Stinky Swamp with all the horrible Craggy Crows," Sophie gasped.

Freya stamped her fairy foot. She looked very determined.

"Don't worry. I'll get it. That wicked old meanie has made me mad!"

Chapter 4
Operation Freya

"You mustn't go into Stinky Swamp, Freya!" cried Sophie.

"It'd be far too dangerous!" gulped Daisy.

Clara looked thoughtful. Being a Clever Fairy, she was good at thinking things through quickly.

"Actually, you're the perfect person to do it, Freya," she said.

"Exactly," nodded Mrs Daffodil. "I know you can do it, Freya. We'll need

everyone to help, though. Here's my plan." She began quietly to explain.

"We'll call it Operation F," Clara grinned. "The F stands for Freya and for Fairy Fightback!"

The four friends were soon ready. They hugged each other, and then Mrs Daffodil took Sophie, Daisy and Clara off to gather together each and every fairy in the school.

"While Freya goes into Stinky Swamp we must try to stop humans noticing that things are going grey," Mrs Daffodil explained. When everybody had understood, she opened the school doors and the little fairies streamed out.

They were all carrying their backpacks full of spells, ready to help.

Everybody did their best to distract any humans who might be about to peer too closely at a grey flower or a little animal that had lost its colour. Sophie used her Magic Beauty Jewel to conjure up pretty music that made people wander away, tapping their feet.

Daisy used her Magic Beauty Jewel to make flashes of dazzling starlight appear in the sky. It made people look up instead of down.

Meanwhile, Clara the Clever Fairy carried on using her Magic Beauty Jewel to turn the grey flowers and little animals back to their true colours. But, as fast as she turned one back, a different one lost its colour. Drizzle's bad magic was still slowly spreading.

"I hope Freya is quick," she thought. She knew Freya was the right fairy for the job, but she was worried about her friend. After all, Drizzle hated fairies. What if she caught one sneaking near her potion?

Freya was trying not to think about that at all, as she flew Shimmerwing to the edge of Stinky Swamp.

"Stay here and keep hidden until I get back," she told the little butterfly. She left him safely under a bush and went on alone.

Stinky Swamp was murky and misty. It had lots of dead tree stumps sticking up like rotten teeth in a sea of green mud that plopped and gurgled.

"Pooh! It smells yucky!" Freya muttered. "Oh well, here goes."

Because Freya was a Fashion Fairy, she had a very special skill. She could camouflage herself to match her surroundings! That's why Clara and Mrs Daffodil had thought she'd be so perfect for creeping into Drizzle's lair. She stood quietly and concentrated hard, until gradually she turned a greeny-browny colour all over. Soon it was impossible to see her against the swampy background.

"Time to find this pongy potion," she murmured.

As she got closer to the middle of the swamp she could hear Drizzle cackling:

"Ha, ha, ha! I hate colour!

I want the world to look much duller!"

"A world turned grey? No way!" Freya muttered, and she flew towards the witch's bubbling cauldron.

Chapter 5
A Spell for Stinky Swamp

The Craggy Crows were sitting on a ring of tree stumps around the cauldron. Freya flew quietly through a gap between two of them, her camouflage magically changing as she went so that she was invisible the whole time. The crows had no idea a fairy had just flown right under their beaks!

Drizzle was flying around the cauldron, dropping in rotten eggs. Freya swooped down and crouched in the cauldron's

shadow. The awful smell made her feel like coughing, but she tried really hard to keep quiet. One little cough, and Drizzle would know an enemy had arrived!

Ever so gently, Freya lifted a small glass bottle from her pocket. Mrs Daffodil had given it to her at school, and had also given her a warning. Freya remembered her words:

"Take this enchanted bottle and fly over the potion in the cauldron, but whatever you do, don't touch it. It'll turn you grey all over, and your camouflage will disappear!"

Freya knew she had to hold the bottle over the top of Drizzle's potion and sing a special spell. This had all sounded quite easy back in Mrs Daffodil's office, but now the little Fashion Fairy was getting nervous. What if the potion splashed on her and Drizzle saw her? She'd have to fly away as fast as she could, right through all the Craggy Crows!

She took a long, deep breath. "Okay, here goes…"

She delved once more into her backpack and, this time, took out a handful of her Fashion Fairy Clever Weather Dust. Holding the magic bottle in one hand and the dust in the other, she flew up above the cauldron. She blew the dust into the air, and a glittering rainbow flashed into the sky over Stinky Swamp.

"Aaaargh! Who put that horrible colour in my sky?" Drizzle screamed, staring upwards.

Freya looked down into the cauldron,

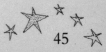

and promptly wished she hadn't. The stinky potion was bubbling and gurgling below her.

"Okay, no time to lose," she murmured to herself. Quietly, she whispered the spell Mrs Daffodil had taught her:

"Fill the bottle to the top,
When it's full, you can stop."

Gloop! Splosh! The potion spat and shook below her. Then a thin stream rose up like a ribbon and flowed straight into the bottle. Once it was full, a tiny bottletop appeared and screwed itself on tightly.

Drizzle was pointing angrily at the rainbow as the Craggy Crows flapped around in a panic.

"Who did this? Find them – NOW!"

"I'd better get out of here," thought Freya. She slipped the precious bottle into her backpack and flew between the dim-witted crows. The potion had not touched her, and she was still camouflaged so perfectly that nobody noticed her.

"Goodbye Stinky Swamp, and good riddance!" she muttered.

Her faithful butterfly, Shimmerwing, was still hiding under a bush on the edge of Stinky Swamp, waiting anxiously for her return. As Freya climbed on his back they heard the Craggy Crows squawking behind them, and Drizzle going crazy.

"There's a fairy in the swamp! Look everywhere! I want you to catch her!"

"We'd better get back to school, Shimmerwing. And fast!" Freya cried.

Chapter 6

Mrs Daffodil's Secret

Shimmerwing could fly much faster than Freya could on her own. Without the butterfly, the Craggy Crows would probably have caught up with the little fairy on her way back. But, luckily for Freya, her pet made sure that she arrived swiftly and safely back at the Utterly Flutterly Fairy School.

Straight away, Freya rushed to find Mrs Daffodil to hand her the enchanted bottle full of Drizzle's potion.

"Well done, Freya! I knew you could do it," Mrs Daffodil clapped delightedly. "Now *I* must get to work!" She pointed to a mysterious box on her desk.

"This is my potion recipe machine," she explained.

Freya was a bit surprised. "Oh, right. Er, it doesn't really look like a machine…"

It was true that the box looked plain, and it was even a bit battered and dusty. But then Mrs Daffodil revealed its secret. The top and sides folded down cleverly. Inside there were lots of tubes and bowls connected up to each other, and they glowed gold!

Mrs Daffodil sat in front of the recipe machine and poured some of Drizzle's potion into one of the golden bowls. Then she sat back and waited.

"It'll take a little while, but eventually it will work out exactly how Drizzle made her potion to turn things grey. Then it'll make an antidote."

"A what-i-dote?" Freya asked.

"An antidote. It means a cure. The machine will make its own potion that we can use to reverse the effects of Drizzle's bad magic."

There was an urgent knock at the door. In burst Clara, Sophie and Daisy.

"It's no good! It's getting worse outside," cried Sophie.

Clara sighed, "The trees are beginning to go grey."

"The humans are bound to notice that!" Daisy added unhappily.

"Not to worry. We'll have the answer in a tinkle," Mrs Daffodil reassured them. A bell rang in the recipe machine and a secret compartment flew open. There was a small golden pot inside.

"Just what we need," Mrs Daffodil smiled. She flew outside, and the whole school looked on anxiously as she held open the little pot and said a spell in a sing-songy voice:

"Where Drizzle's potion made things grey,
Now turn them back the other way."

Tiny gold stars spilled out of the pot and floated off into the sky.

"That's an antidote," Freya explained proudly to her friends.

"A what-i-dote?" Daisy asked.

"Let's just say, it'll make everything alright,' laughed Freya.

Sure enough, as the little golden stars spread out, colour flooded back into everything that had gone grey.

Clara hugged Freya. "Phew! The panic's over, thanks to you. Let's go back inside and do something really quiet and stress-free for the rest of the day!"

Freya sighed with relief. "Thank goodness everything has got back to normal."

But she had spoken too soon. Back in the clothes shop in the human town, a little girl was gazing at the new treasure she'd found on the shelf – Freya's Magic Beauty Jewel! She rubbed it gently with her finger to make it sparkle...

Chapter 7
A Mighty Muddle

The little girl was looking out of the window when she rubbed Freya's beauty jewel, and the minute she did it, strange things began to happen. Because the jewel did Fashion Fairy magic, it changed people's clothes!

A man walking past outside suddenly found that, instead of wearing smart black shoes, he was shuffling along in pink fluffy slippers. Some people found their clothes shrinking. Some found

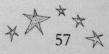

themselves wearing things that were now far too big.

The little girl had no idea what she'd done, and why people seemed to be getting cross outside in the street. She went off to the park to play, taking the jewel with her in her pocket.

The park-keeper was standing by the pond in his overalls when the little girl walked past. She popped her hand into her pocket to find a sweet, and accidentally touched the jewel. Suddenly, the park-keeper's outfit changed completely. He looked down and found he was wearing a ballet tutu! He was so surprised, he tripped over and fell into the pond.

Some park workmen were putting up a new climbing frame nearby when the little girl once again touched the jewel.

The next thing they knew, they were all
wearing clown outfits, with giant shoes,
funny hats and false noses!

Meanwhile, back in Stinky Swamp, Drizzle's potion had lost all its power once again. With no upset or muddle in the human world, it had stopped bubbling, and Drizzle was looking even more sour-faced than usual, because she couldn't make any more bad magic.

Then suddenly, without any warning, the potion began to bubble up again.

Gloop! Pop!

"Well, well, well!" Drizzle cackled. "Some muddle must be happening in the human town, and we didn't even have to start it ourselves!"

GLOOP!

SPLOSH!

The potion began to bubble and splash harder, because the more the little girl touched Freya's jewel, the more people found their clothes changing, and the angrier they got.

She was making a mighty muddle and it was making Drizzle's potion ever more powerful!

The Utterly Flutterly Fairies had no idea what was happening until nearly home time, when the little girl arrived with her mum at the human school's gates, to pick up her big brother. As the teachers and schoolchildren came out into the playground, she reached into her pocket and her fingers tightened around the jewel.

The sounds of laughter and grumbling soon drifted up to the fairy school.

"Hey! Something's going on outside!" Sophie said, looking out of the window.

Some humans had found themselves suddenly wearing their coats on back-to-front. Everyone else had funny hats on! Some people were getting cross. Others were pointing at each other and giggling.

Freya was puzzled. "How could somebody change clothes unless they had a Fashion Fairy Beauty Jewel? Oh no!"

She scrambled to open her backpack, and hunted frantically inside.

"Somebody down there has my beauty jewel!" she cried.

Clara pointed. "That little girl over there is the only person who isn't wearing something strange. I'm guessing it's her," she said. "Isn't her mum the lady from the clothes shop?"

"Of course! I must have left my jewel there!" Freya moaned.

Mrs Daffodil came up behind them. "I'll sort out the clothes mess here. You go and get your jewel back," she said.

Freya pulled a face. "I'd better be quick, before the whole town turns into one big fashion disaster!"

Chapter 8
Thank You, Fairies

Clara frowned. "We have to think of a way to get the little girl to give us the jewel. I don't think we should steal it from her."

Sophie nodded. "You're right."

The four friends sat thinking hard. Then Freya jumped up.

"This little girl likes shiny, pretty things, just like me, right? What if we give her some butterfly clips as a swap for my Magic Beauty Jewel?"

Clara nodded. "That sounds good, but how? We can't just ask her. Remember the first rule of the school? Never let a human see you."

Freya explained her idea. "First, I'll need everybody's clips. Sorry, but I'll make you all some more if I get my jewel back."

Everyone gave her back their pretty butterfly clips and Freya put them in a box. She wrote a sign:

FOR SALE
Teeny-tiny butterfly clips
for your doll.
Price: one jewel.

The four friends rushed off to the clothes shop in the human town, carrying the box between them. They spotted the little girl outside in the garden. She was sitting on a blanket, having a tea party with her doll.

"Perfect!" Freya grinned. They put the box by a flowerpot and hid nearby.

"Now it's my turn for some spell-making," smiled Clara. She put on her Clever Fairy Good Feeling Spell Ring. It was full of special magic for giving people bright ideas. Then she stared hard at the little girl, who stood up and turned towards the flowerpot.

"I've had a good idea. I'll use that pot to decorate our picnic blanket," she said to her doll.

"She's coming over!" squealed Daisy excitedly.

"Oh, what's this?" The little girl saw

the box, looked closely at it and read the sign.

"I'd like those clips for my doll," she murmured. She felt in her pocket and brought out Freya's missing magic jewel. She popped it in the box, and took out the clips.

"Yes! It worked!" Freya cried.

FOR SALE
Teeny-tiny butterfly clips
for your doll.
Price: one jewel

"Sssh!" Sophie warned. "She mustn't know we're here!"

"Hmm," Daisy murmured in a thoughtful voice. Being a Dream Fairy she knew that, although humans could never see fairies, often they still believed in them. She had a feeling that the little girl might know who'd made the tiny clips.

When the girl had turned away, Freya rushed over and grabbed her jewel.

"Right! I'd better sort out all those messed-up outfits!" she declared, and the four fairies flew away to get busy.

When they had gone, the little girl went back to the box, and saw that it was empty.

"Thank you, fairies," she smiled.

Daisy had been right. The little girl did believe in fairies!

After all, don't you?

Chapter 9
Freya Sorts it Out

Freya and her friends flew around the human town, staying hidden behind lampposts or up on rooftops. Freya concentrated hard, clutching her beauty jewel tightly, and using its magic to sort out any muddled-up clothing nearby. Her friends helped to spot funny outfits that needed her attention.

She couldn't help giggling a little bit at the silly sights the little girl had made happen. "Mmm, pink slippers! I'm not

sure they're a great look for everyone!"

The man in the pink slippers was very glad to get his proper shoes back, and everyone was pleased to find their clothes fitted them again.

Over in the park, the park-keeper's ballet tutu turned back into an overall, much to his relief. He'd been hiding away in his shed, feeling very embarrassed and wondering how he was going to get home wearing a ballet costume.

Freya made the clowns' outfits disappear too, though the workmen had actually quite enjoyed being clowns for a while and making everybody laugh.

When they had finished putting everything right, the four friends sat down for a well-earned rest under a hedge in the park.

"Did you put *everything* back the way it was before?" Clara asked.

"Yes, well…*nearly* everything," Freya grinned. "I *am* a Fashion Fairy, after all. I did make one or two tiny improvements to some outfits. They were good ones, though!" No wonder the park-keeper found a few extra useful pockets in his overalls, and the workmen found they all had brand new, shiny boots.

"Fairies, fairies, where are you?" a soft voice called. It was Mrs Daffodil out looking for them, to explain what she'd done and make sure that all the mess was sorted out.

"I've cast a spell to make the humans forget that this fashion muddle ever happened. But the mix-ups will have made Drizzle's potion powerful again. I'm afraid she'll be back to do some more mischief."

Freya shook her head firmly. "Not if I have anything to do with it! I've had enough of that miserable old grumpypants for a while, and I'm not scared of her any more! I'll sort her out. You wait and see!"

Chapter 10
Drizzle Gets a Makeover

Freya rushed home to speak to Shimmerwing.

"We've got to go back to Stinky Swamp, one more time. But this time it won't be so scary, because I know just what to expect," she explained. So, once again, they flew together to the edge of the swamp.

"Wait here. I won't be long, I promise," she told her pet. He folded his wings to wait patiently under the bushes once more.

Freya again used her camouflage magic to turn herself a mixture of mouldy-looking green and muddy-looking brown – the colours of Stinky Swamp. She flew straight past the stupid Craggy Crows and landed on a tree stump to watch Drizzle from a safe distance.

Drizzle was flying around her cauldron, screeching,

"My potion is bubbling nicely! I'm going to pour a bucketful of it over the human town and show them who's boss. I'll make them all wear dull clothes. Everything will be dull, dull, dull. There'll be no colour anywhere, and all the world will be wonderfully witchy!"

She clapped her warty hands together with glee.

"This time I'll make so much mess with my magic, that Daffodil won't be able to clean it up, ever. I will rule the world, witch-style!"

"I don't think so, you old bootface!"
Freya muttered. She clutched her
Fashion Fairy Beauty Jewel in her hand
and stared hard at Drizzle.

Suddenly, the witch's dull, horrible
outfit transformed! For a start, it turned
lots of different colours, thanks to Freya's

fashion magic. Drizzle found herself wearing a blue spotty top and a striped red and yellow skirt with frills on it. Her shoes were gold, her stockings were lilac, and her hat was the brightest pink you could ever imagine. It had silver bells on top that tinkled whenever she moved.

She looked so funny and bright that the Craggy Crows began to snigger at her.

She squealed wildly.

"Noooo! I can't let anybody see me like this! Think of my image – it'll ruin my witchy reputation forever!"

"Exactly. Serves you right," Freya muttered, and she zipped back out of Stinky Swamp to find Shimmerwing, who carried her home to her beautiful, colourful garden.

Drizzle didn't dare leave Stinky Swamp until her clothes went back to normal, and they didn't change for ages. By the time she looked witchy again, her potion had lost all its power. It had stopped bubbling and was completely useless for anything.

"It's surprising we haven't heard or seen Drizzle. I was expecting more trouble," Mrs Daffodil remarked one day at school. Freya grinned, and explained what she'd done.

"Let's just say she's having a bad fashion moment," she giggled. "I gave her a makeover she'll never forget. It was magic!"

Utterly Flutterly Quiz

What's your fairy fashion style? Try our Utterly Flutterly Fairy fashion quiz to find out!

1. Your dream outfit would be:

A. A princess ball gown, tiara and sparkly necklace
B. Jeans and your favourite T-shirt
C. A colourful mini dress with glittery tights
D. A designer top and skirt with gold jewellery

2. What are your favourite accessories?

A. Pretty bags, pink nail varnish and anything glittery
B. Beads, colourful bracelets and cool belts
C. Scarves, long necklaces and brightly coloured shoes
D. Large bags, big sunglasses and stylish hats

3. Which of these do you like wearing the most?

A. Pretty skirts
B. Comfy trousers
C. Cool dresses
D. Skinny jeans

4. What colours do you wear the most?

A. Pink and pastel colours
B. Blue, with some bright colours thrown in
C. Purple, green and silver
D. Whatever's in fashion – you love to wear this season's colour

5. Which would be your perfect pair of shoes?

A. Pink platforms with a sparkly strap
B. Funky trainers
C. Metallic gold sandals with a cute heel
D. Trendy fleece-lined boots

Utterly Flutterly Quiz Answers

Now check your answers to find out what your fairy fashion style is:

Mostly As: Your style is ultra girly — you love pinks, pastels and anything glittery or fluffy.

Mostly Bs: Your style is relaxed and casual, but you add bright, funky accessories so you always look cool.

Mostly Cs: Your style is super-imaginative — you love to mix and match styles and patterns. You're a real trendsetter.

Mostly Ds: You're a true fashionista! You always keep up to date with what celebs are wearing and you're mega trendy.

84

Utterly Flutterly Anagrams

Drizzle the Wicked Witch has been causing mischief by muddling up these words so that no one can read them. Can you sort them out and work out what they should say? Turn the page upside down to see if you're right.

treflutby

yarfe

worbain

locseth hops

roluco

isafnho

wrignemmshi

tiantode

prontioae f

glamcafoue

Answers:

treflutby: butterfly, *yarfe:* freya, *worbain:* rainbow,
locseth hops: clothes shop, *roluco:* colour, *isafnho:* fashion,
wrignemmshi: shimmerwing, *tiantode:* antidote,
prontioae f: operation f, *glamcafoue:* camouflage

Butterfly cakes

Freya travels to fairy school on her pet butterfly, Shimmerwing. Can you guess what her favourite party food might be?

Ingredients
Makes approx 16

110g/4oz caster sugar
110g/4oz butter or margarine
75g/3oz self-raising flour
2 medium-sized eggs
A few drops of vanilla extract

Ingredients for the icing

175g/6oz icing sugar
75g/3oz unsalted butter
A few drops of vanilla extract
Milk or warm water
Icing sugar to dust

Kit

Paper baking cases, baking tray, knife, metal spoon, mixing bowl, sieve, wooden spoon

Sponge

1. Preheat the oven to 180°C/350F/Gas Mark 4. Cream together the butter and sugar until fluffy.

2. Gradually beat in the eggs and the vanilla extract. If the mixture starts to curdle, add a little flour.

3. Fold in the flour, using a metal spoon.

4. Place spoonfuls of the mixture into baking cases and bake for 15–20 minutes, then take them out of the oven and leave them to cool.

REMEMBER! ALWAYS ASK AN ADULT TO HELP YOU WHEN USING THE OVEN!

Icing

Place the butter in a bowl and beat until soft. Gradually sift and beat in the icing sugar. Mix in a few drops of vanilla extract and enough milk or water to make the icing fluffy and spreadable.

To decorate

1. Ask an adult to help you carefully cut a circle out of the top of each cake.

2. Cut each circle in half and set aside.

3. Fill the hole in the top of each cake with the vanilla butter icing.

4. Place the two half circles of cake on top to resemble butterfly wings, as shown.

5. Dust the top of each cake lightly with icing sugar.

How to make a friendship bracelet

Why not make some beautiful friendship bracelets to give to your best friends? Just follow the step-by-step instructions below.

You will need:

⭐ *embroidery thread in three colours*
⭐ *scissors*

1. Take three long pieces of thread and tie them together at one end, as shown.

2. Place the tied-up end under something heavy to keep it in place. This will help you to pull the threads tight.

3. Plait the three pieces of coloured thread as if you were plaiting your hair.

4. When your plait is long enough to fit easily around your wrist, tie the ends together. Neaten both ends by cutting off any extra thread.

Fairy code words!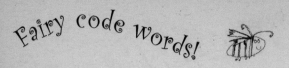

You can make up fairy code words by taking each letter from a word and using it to start another word like this:

Fabulous

Radiant

Elegant

Your friend

Adorable

Funky

Admirable

Stylish

Hip

Inventive

Original

New

Sparkly

Happy

Irresistible

Marvellous

Magical

Extraordinary

Rainbow-like

Winged

Impressive

Nimble

Glittering

More word ideas!

Why don't you try making up a fairy code word using your own name? Here are some words to get you started:

Cheerful

Loving

Magical

Funny

Pretty

Energetic

Interesting

Brilliant

Quirky

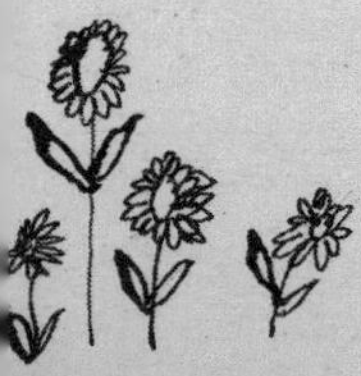

How to make a butterfly clip

You will need:

- ✦ an old hair clip
- ✦ glue
- ✦ card
- ✦ scissors
- ✦ glitter
- ✦ colouring pens
- ✦ double-sided tape

1. Fold a piece of card in half and draw a half butterfly shape on one side. Your shape can be any size, depending on how big your clip is.

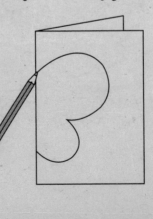

2. Ask an adult to help you to carefully cut out the shape, as shown.

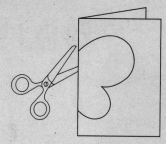

3. Unfold the card to reveal a butterfly shape and decorate using colouring pens, glitter and glue.

4. Stick your butterfly to an old hair clip, as shown, using double-sided tape.

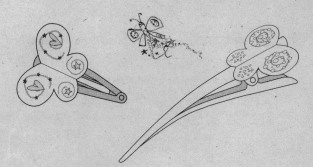

5. Wear your butterfly clip in your hair or pinned to your clothes, to add glamour to your outfit.

Look out for these
Utterly Flutterly titles!

Utterly Flutterly Fairies

Sophie
the
Birthday Fairy

Moira Butterf...

Utterly Flutterly Fairies

Clara
the
Clever Fairy

Moira Butt...

Utterly Flutterly Fairies

Daisy
the
Dream Fairy

Moira Butterfield